ALPHA

Book 1

Long Nights and Magic Coffee

Alpha

BY ORA FONTAY

From the series:

Long Nights And Magic Coffee

By Ora Fontay

Intro

Calm Communication

Val laid across the bed facing her sliding closet doors that are also mirrors. She smiled, then winked at herself before slowly draping her feet to the floor. She swayed towards the light of the sun, pulled back the drapes, opened the window and inhaled deeply. The heat from the sun's rays tickled her skin and she welcomed it. She pushed her head closer to the window admiring her magical forest as she beautifully named it. It featured hand painted rocks, exotic flowers of vibrant colors, two pine trees and one weeping willow which gave off the sweetest aroma and energy. Val made sure to plant the pine trees close to her window, otherwise Duluth, Georgia's air sometimes carried a disgust of congestion and dysfunctional smog. She closed her eyes and focused on box breathing- pines and possibilities. Her mind went back to her traditional childhood-something she'd grown to despise and sometimes forget. She remembered the day her fraternal twin passed away in the hands of her pastor and so called church family. They were so busy believing Jesus would fix it that they neglected the obvious-he wouldn't and couldn't. Victor and Valerie were thick as thieves, the best of friends and four minute apart fraternal twins. A growling frown crossed her face as she exhaled into the memory of her family standing in the lines for free food, shelter and financial assistance because her mother had given all their bill money to the church believing it would be blessed with a tenfold return. Andrea Joy was a die hard Christian going to every service, every concert, and every bible study, but still struggled on every hand. She never understood how her mother could serve someone who didn't lookout for his people. A tear fell as Val reflected on the day everything changed. She and Victor were sitting in church listening to the preacher stand in the sanctified pulpit and instill fear, guilt, and hope into the congregation. He'd warn them of not being able to buy their way into heaven, but still give tithes and offerings because this would ensure their name is written in the book of life. Before the pastor could finish the statement they started running down the aisle placing hundreds of bills into the circular gold pans. Every hand that touched it screamed how their life will never be the same. No one realized how true that statement would ring. Andrea scrambled through her purse looking for whatever dollar bills she had. She counted out seven then got up to run, but Victor stopped her in her tracks as he held his chest.His eyes looked desperate and his energy seemed drained. Val looked at her bestie and grabbed his small frame into a hug. Victor didn't try to push Val off like normal and Andrea began screaming. Everyone turned from shouting to speaking in tongues. The pastor warned that they all were about to witness a miracle. He came over with his blessed oil and thumb pressing Victor's head demanding the devil to leave. Val screamed for someone to call an ambulance. She was only 7- didn't know much- but she knew prayer of exorcism wasn't the answer. They ignored her as their tongue speaking and oil drippings became unbearable as Val did the unimaginable. She pulled him from the hands of everyone and they took off running. He tried to stay with her but suddenly collapsed. His heart stopped and magically so did all the prayers.The pastor then says, the lord giveth and taketh, praise and bless the lord. Val heard a large thump hit the floor. She turned to discover her mother passed out and she swiftly followed. The ambulance was finally called.

Val's eyes began blinking rapidly before focusing on being in a hospital bed with an IV pumping something she couldn't understand or pronounce. Her mom was lying in the next bed sleeping so Val began begging everyone within earshot and eyesight for Victor's whereabouts, but they remained silent only shaking their heads back and forth. She looked past everyone to see anyone that looked like Victor and saw her dad standing tall and strong. As soon as their eyes connected his strength depleted. He wanted to fold over, but walked over slowly and explained everything that happened, but she couldn't hear anything over her sorrow. She'd become hysterical with no resolve. A nurse passing by walked in and begged Mr. Joy to allow her to assist. Val tried to refuse service, but the nurse's touch instantly eased her sorrow and calmed her fears. The nurse was beautifully melainated, tall, regal and had a presence of power. She carried a bag labeled 'saline' and swapped it out with the bag Val couldn't pronounce. Once connected she began pressing buttons and clearing out all warnings. She flicked her fingers, thumped the bag twice and gold dust started forming. Before Val could attest the nurse smiled bright forcing Val to turn her face into a sweet slumber. She dreamed of playing with Victor and everything being better than before. Their home- immaculate, their refrigerator -full, their clothes -new with their family harmony on a hunnid! It felt too real to wake up to her greatest nightmare, a life without her twin.. Her youth dragged, until one day it didn't anymore. She grew up and so did everyone else, giving her the life of her dreams.

***

Val wiped the tears from her cheeks with the same finger and flick. She had no time for mourning. She inhaled deep while adoring the pine trees, then exhaled with a high sigh. She desperately needed a picker upper, something to lighten her mood. So, she sniffed her dress hoping she could still smell his scent, and like magic it filled her nostrils. "Why can I still smell him?" she wondered.

Dancing thoughts of her new beau two stepped in her mind. She'd just met him two days ago but instantly felt 'a knowing' he was her forever. The thought of him made her body's temperature rise like nipples. Without warning, her ex lover's face creeped in her mind and her smile instantly vanished. She rolled her eyes while shaking her head disapprovingly. She felt urged to check the order of things, glanced at the window's panel, adjusted her tiger's eye, then waited. Nothing happened so she flopped onto the bed.She did a quick glance at herself and paused. Her eyes were doing that thing again. She'd realized it was happening more frequently and needed answers but who could she turn to for discussion of a topic she couldn't understand enough to discuss?

Ever since the day she decided to mix her crystals with her coffee she's been seeing things, hearing things, and doing things out of the ordinary. She had this bright idea to take her favorite stones: sodalite, angelite, amethyst, and black tourmaline and mix it with her favorite beans. She prayed over it, saged it, spoke some affirmations to it-setting great intentions- then drank it. It was the most delicious cup of coffee she'd ever had. Her lips began smacking as she licked them- getting every inch of flavor- before feeling a jolt shoot through her body. She let out a happy scream then noticed she'd finished the entire cup without one stone left in it. It was like she ignited something, but thought nothing of it until later that night her eyes shined bright as golden flakes floating in the 'saline' labeled bag. Another incident happened while she watched her guilty pleasure of ratchet reality tv accidentally dropping a glass on her foot. Blood trickled from the gash as she pulled out the chunk piece hopping around for a band aid. Before she could reach the bathroom her pain ceased and her skin was healed. She wanted to freak out, but her curiosity was too curious. Over the next couple of months her body went through changes she couldn't explain. She thought the SpiderMan syndrome was indeed unraveling in her own life. She just knew a web was growing between her fingers. She wanted to call her karmic family for clarification but quickly understood every answer needed was always within. She turned to meditation but even that was becoming something intensely close to literally sitting in the clouds. Her body was changing, her eyes were shining, and her strength was increasing. She was becoming someone, or something.

She turned towards the mirror flipping her sister locs up and down until they draped beautifully across her shoulders. She felt a dance coming on and started swaying her shoulders. Her cell phone rang and the biggest smile flashed across her face as his name flashed across her screen. He was everything her ex wasn't, or could ever be. She thought of the depth of their conversations, the time spent talking, the laughs, but especially the lessons-feeling it creates their strong connection and she felt so connected. Their bond was stronger than gorilla glue's hold on hair; 'it don't move!' Val kicked her legs, laid back in a full body stretch and answered.

***

[Val] "It's not funny Jay, stoooop laughing.(hahaha) I'm not even the same behind this. I've lost friends and some of my family thinks I'm crazy, and can you believe it's all because of religion?

[Jay] "Oh wow, religion. I'm intrigued."

[Val] "Nah, for real I'd grown tired of tradition. I just needed a new way, a new perspective, a new path to travel so I gave up being conditioned, controlled and disconnected ya know." She took a sip of her coffee then rested it on the nightstand. "Trying to explain my truth became my greatest mistake. The way they look at me when I enter the room smelling like Florida water, crystallized down, stones dangling, beads bangling-(hahaaahaaa)-they start backing up like I'm a vampire. Where they do that at?."

Jay began laughing. She'd usually snap off thinking one thing that had nothing to do with anything, but his laughter and powerful perspective was bringing joy to her life.

[Jay] "Don't stop now. Tell me more of the shenanigans."

[Val] "You are a whole mess. I'm fussing about you think it's funny. I guess it is kinda funny."

[Jay] "Kinda, woman this is hilarious. Go on, I'm listening."

[Val] "Anywho, they plead the blood while calling me a witch. The crazy part is some of my cousins who don't even go to church had the nerve to call me the devil. Jay, these fools even tried performing an exorcism on me!"

[Jay] "An exorcism? So help me understand this -they believe they have power to remove evil from you, but not 'the devil who's always busy' from their own lives?"

He laughed heartily. His deep tone and vibe was soothing to her. She curled under her blanket finding that comfy spot.She wiggled her toes then giggled like a schoolgirl behind what she was doing.

[Val] "Listen, they just knew something evil would pop outta me and if it did, they would've run in every direction but the right one. I was over it because I'd questioned *why* way too many times. I needed answers and the answers they gave left me with more questions. They choose to believe I'm secretly angry with God. Now I have every right to be angry, but the truth is, I'm only repeating the word. What I practice is in 'their' word, yet they call it blasphemy."

[Jay] "I can't believe they are questioning your belief but not where the religion came from.I learned in high school's history class that our oppressor -an enemy, a hater of this chocolate magic-taught Christianity strictly to justify enslaving our ancestors! I also learned early on in school that every color together makes one exquisite color of black. We are the sole reason why other shades of human exist and they have the nerve to chant purity, march the streets and burn crosses talking about how they want us gone. Shiddd! I don't recall our ancestors freely coming to this place. No matter what anyone says 'we didn't volunteer' for no slave shit! Praising white Jesus wasn't our way of connecting with the Creator before bondage and left up to me, it won't be while free. Our way was natural- grounding with nature-wearing stones-reading omens-burning sage-meditating-tapping into the truth of the land-respecting it."

[Val] "Oooh wee, talk that talk baby!"

[Jay] "Don't make me laugh, woman. I'm trying to learn you something!" He giggled and kept talking. "Our ancestors honored their ancestors. They honored their guides. They understood acknowledging them shaped their power. Hey- I can go on and on about this, but I will dial it back. We have the rest of our lives to talk about the beginning of America and the ending of religion, so allow me to shift. How long have you been on your quest for truth?"

Val bucked her eyes and mouthed 'forever' then loudly exhaled with a smile.

[Val] "First off, you are speaking truth sir! I'm snapping my fingers and toes on that note. Okayyyy- she cleared her throat-let me focus. I've been on this quest since 2011. I've had some strange things happen along the way, but that's another subject for another time. I mean, we do have forever." She snickered but kept talking. "Everything I mentioned earlier became my medicine along with self love and shadow work. Ya know what tho -the greatest of all is affirmations-freaking life changing when you speak life. The path ain't without obstacles, but ya know-she shroud her shoulders- I'm walking it."

[Jay] "You're doing amazing. Hey, I'm glad I met you at this phase of the journey."

[Val] "Jay, you're making me blush. I can't believe we just met days ago. It feels like I've known-

[Jay] "Me forever huh! I feel the same."

They shared a laugh.

[Val] "So now you're completing my sentences. You know what this means.

[Jay] "No, tell me Ms. V."

[Va] "Ms. V- I like that. It means-" She suddenly felt anxious and stood up from the bed. She looked around the room searching for something, or someone. She didn't know what exactly, but she knew something wasn't right. "Hey, I hate bringing up my ex while talking with my next, but he's become really strange. It's like he's stalking me or something. I don't know why I-well I know why- but-maybe I'm just being-hmm ya know what, never mind."

[Jay] "I know exactly what you mean and if I'm right- you felt something, didn't you?"

Val snatched the phone from her ear and looked into it strangely.

She wondered how he knew, but dared not ask to avoid opening a can she desired to keep closed. Jay sensed her hesitation, but pushed the issue anyway.

[Jay] "That's a serious matter Val. Do I need to come and guard you? I have no quarrels with that!"

Val thought about him being there and smiled from her heart. She couldn't deny she wanted him near her. The thought of laying next to him made her relax and slightly moan.

[Jay] "What was that? Is that a yes-a quiet one, but a yes?"

She smiled wide, then responded with great confidence.

[Val] "I'm okay. I can handle myself just fine. Besides, the next time we connect I have something important to share with you that could change the trajectory of us. So, if ya wouldn't mind our next convo I'd love to sit and discuss. Also, I make a mean cup of coffee that'll change your life."

[Jay] "Woman, I only drink the finest." He chuckled, waiting for a reaction.

[Val] "That's awesome man because I only brew the finest. I bet you'll love every bean that touches your pallet."

[Jay] "You kiss yo momma with that mouth!"

Val laughed so hard she began choking. Her laughter spread like rumors and he was soon infected with joy.

-(Knock...knock..knock)

[Val] "Ohhh-someone's at the door. It's probably Trish. We're having a grown woman play date. I will call you back when I can."

(Bang- bang...BANG!!) She hung up and ran to the door.

[Val] "Hold ya mule gal, I'm coming!"

[Josh] "Open the door! I know you're in there!"

***

Chapter 1

Judge and Jury

September 2017

She stood on the other side wondering why she didn't take Jay up on the offer. Josh's knocks went from nice taps to urgent bangs but she could care less. She stepped to the door deeply sighing and giving herself a glance in the mirror. She saw her eyes do that thing again, but this time it scattered her breathing. She clutched her chest then made a mental note to talk with her babalola about what she's been experiencing.

Adjusting the black tourmaline crystal stuffed between her breasts she was prepared to tell him it's over, but he had other plans. Before she could invite him in he'd force entry using her neck as his compass guide throughout the hallway. Her eyes bucked as her breathing waxed desperate..

Everything in his path was destroyed including her newly purchased Jacobb Lawrence paintings.

[Josh] "Why you playing games? You heard me knocking? Talllkkkk!"

Val couldn't think, talk, or breathe so she just surrendered and slumped. He let go and her face bounced from the floor as her head hit the wall. Stars were everywhere, but it wasn't nightfall. She sprawled her body across the floor, inhaled deeply, then tried standing up. She stumbled a bit, but used her shoulder and wall for better balance.

[Val] "What the entire fuck is wrong with you? Your energy is so off."

He snatched her small frame in one hand. Again, holding her neck, but this time he covered her mouth. She squirmed constantly to find relief. Infuriated with her struggle, he spat in her face and cursed the day she was born. Every drop of his hot saliva touched her forehead as virulent venom. He laughed but stopped abruptly when her entire body went stiff like a statue. He almost stopped, but just as soon as it came it left, so he tightened his grip around her neck and continued his rant.

[Josh] "You double crossing slut! I was trying desperately to reach you, but you didn't answer the phone. You didn't respond to my text, hell-you didn't even acknowledge my damn bat signal, but you wanna talk about energy. I tried loving you the way you wanted but you rejected me, found fault in everything I did. So you can die slow hoe. You and your fucking stones areeeee..."

His voice faded as his eyes became fixated on the biggest amethyst crystal he'd ever seen. It was oddly shaped and shining bearing metallic colors of purple, yellow, and turquoise as a hummingbird hovered the top. It was big enough to step in and just be. Josh was hypnotized and for a slight moment of time he'd forgotten foolery and felt optimistic. He pointed to the crystal.

[Josh] "Where did you get this from?" He forced her neck in the direction of the amethyst. "You hear me talking to you. Where did you get this?"

When she didn't respond he realized his neck grip was obstructing her speech. With a half-smile he removed his hand from her mouth and loosened his grip. Her once pearly whites were now blood stained. She coughed hard and deep before catching her breath's rhythm. He relaxed his grip even more, giving her time to inwardly chant '*OM*'. Within moments she was able to feel the present power of her ancestors and spirit guides.

[Val] "I got it from the store we went to. You know that store that you claimed I spent way too much money in. You remember?"

She knew she couldn't do anything physically to hurt him, but mentally things were lining up for her escape. At least she'd hoped so. She was deep in thought when his back hand crossed her face reminding her that he was there for unpleasant business. The taste of warm blood trickled down her throat. She closed her eyes and sucked her lips tight to refrain from an outward scream. However, inwardly her scream shattered all the glass in the house.

[Josh] "I believed all that energy shit you were talking bout just as you believe there's a way to get out of this. Surprise, it ain't one! You conniving bitch-you deserve everything coming your way." He kicked over the crystal he'd just admired. It crashed onto the hardwood floor, but shockingly it didn't shatter. This angered him even more, but scared him too. "Got me chanting and sage'n. I got all these rocks, crystals-whateva you wanna call em-in my car, my house and not one kept me from fucking you up right now. See how stupid this shit is? Might as well gone back to Jesus. Maybe he can take the wheel before you hit this brick wall."

He was out for blood and used his nails to dig into her neck to get it. Remaining resolute in her strength, she sucked in her lips and said nothing.

[Josh] "Oooh you're tough now?"

A smile crept across his face as he reflected on their first encounter.

Time stood still as he gazed upon her beauty from across the room. He could see she was a force to be reckoned with and he was all about wrecking shit. She stood 5'3 in height but he could tell she was a giant in everything else. Her body made him drool and quiver. It wasn't what he was accustomed to, but something triggered him and he needed to shoot his shot. He eyeballed her little booty in the yellow camouflage pants that hugged her mid-size waist. He let his eyes travel to her breast and was pleased at how nicely large they were. Though it wasn't what he was used to, her stance made her body seem perfect to him.

She wore her usual style of waist beads, bangles, no bra and off shoulders halters with one word expressing her mood for the day. Her makeup included the usual glossy lips, heavy mascara and gold eyeshadow complimenting her brown and sunflower colored eyes. Her sil-

ver and black locs that normally drape her shoulders were pinned in an updo full of colorful pearls, black onyx and opals shaped as a crown. But the icing on the cake for Josh was her Hershey's chocolate skin. It was smooth and he wanted to taste its sweetness. Her aroma carried a scent of what he believed heaven must smell like. She was magnetic - majestic and he needed to get next to her hoping someday to get under and on top of her. She was his preference and his picture of perfection. Her presence spoke eloquence and grace and he was in awe. But, she never looked his way. Her head stayed down as she focused on the vending machine of 'Mess in A Bottle' waiting patiently to select her purchase, but he was anxious and jumped the line.

*[**Josh**] "Excuse me, but what shirt do you think would be a good fit for me? I'm having a hard time making up my mind."*

Without looking up, she gave the surface advice to get "what you want". She pushed a button and out popped her shirt telling her to rule shit. His genuine laughter caught her attention. Once they locked eyes, he locked on the charm and stepped into her personal space - leaving her literally with no room to say no.

*[**Josh**] "So, I had to laugh for you to notice me. Do you see men as jokes or something?"*

She backed up a little, getting back her personal space.

*[**Val**] "I acknowledge vibrations and frequencies. Is it my fault you're undetectable? You gotta ignite, alert, ring my alarm-do something-otherwise I can't see you."*

***

For a moment he thought he'd forgive her latest betrayal and hear her out. Once he looked down upon her frowned face he was over being kind. He used great force to knee her in the chest causing her body to jerk forward as she bellowed louder than he'd anticipated. She fell over and he allowed her body to osculate the floor.

[Val] "Don't hurt me! I need to tell you something, pluu------- .

He forced his hand over her mouth and 3 of her top and bottom teeth met the fat of his hand. She'd grown tired of playing victim and became irritated for having been cast in the role she never signed up to play. Damsel in distress was a job she'd decline even if it were the only job. Excruciating pain shot throughout his body as she tried forcefully to make her teeth touch. He yanked his hand from her mouth's grip and jabbed her in the chest. She walked through his punch and charged him, forcing her fingers and nails into his eyes. He fell backwards.

[Josh] "You bitch!"

She took off running down the hallway towards the kitchen. He tried dragging her back, but she wiggled from his grip and reached the kitchen's island. He was on her heels and grabbed her ankle pulling her down. Her face and forehead kissed the floor again with a smack. Again, she walked through it and began throwing everything inside the dishwasher onto the floor. She needed a fort and that was the only thing close. Crashes of plates and utensils hit the floor musically. She looked up remembering her hanging skillets. She hurried to grab it but lost its grip and the cast iron skillet swivel danced before falling flat. She moaned in pain as she moved towards it. She grabbed the skillet and swung hard, connecting with his fingers and head. Immediately, he covered his face with his arms. She swung again hitting his elbow. He tried pushing her off, but she only grew stronger. He used his body to push her off then kicked her hard forcing her back into the stove. She cringed in pain but her adrenaline shot through the roof causing pain to transfer as fuel. He gathered all his strength and stood. She wasn't afraid of his body towering her - fight mode was activated.

[Josh] "Bring yo ass and see what I do!"

His right eye leaked blood-filled tears. He charged, then punched her into the refrigerator causing the door to fly open and its door contents to crash to the floor. Shattered glass hit the floor and her bare feet, but she felt nothing. She tried pushing him away, but he punched her again-this time knocking her to the floor and the glass into her right cheek. Blood began running from her face. She blinked her eyes and when she opened again, he was kneeling over her. She turned her face and swung the skillet, hitting him in the temple. He squalled and dropped to the floor. She swung until his hands fell on the sides of his body leaving his face exposed. She kept swinging at his bare face until he fell quiet. Sweat dripped from her body like she was standing in a shower. Her words came just as wet.

[Val] "You think you can just come up in my house and disrespect me? You must have lost your damn mind. I'm not with all this violent shit but you're pushing me over the edge."

Her breath became sprightly and hard as her energy depleted fast. She dropped the skillet and screamed in frustration.

[Val] "Now that you got some sense about yourself I need to tell you something important, so stop the bullshit so we can talllllk. Do you hear me? Josh!!"

He didn't respond or move.

[Val] "Okay, so you think this shit is funny. Get up! You got some damn nerve storming up in my home choking the prana from my being and for what? For whatttt? And now you have the audacity to give me the silent treatment, ME of all people. Getcho ass up Josh! I saw your text, the pictures, the bullshit- I promise you can leave forever after I say what the fucc I need to say."

She looked over and screamed like a banshee.

[Val] "Noooo, no no noooooo please get up! What the fuccccc!"

She looked around for support, but all she saw was disaster. Her eyes fell back to Josh.

[Val] "Look at what you made me do!"

Desperate knocks disrupted her whining. She got quiet and laid flat on top of him now close enough to see the destruction of her rage. His brains slowly seeped onto her freshly mopped floor. She gagged then vomited on his body. The knocks went from normal taps to banging, kicking and hard pounding. She looked down to ensure Josh was still there because she didn't need to experience no ground hog repeat this day shit. Val's name rang from the other side of the door like a song. She perked up once she heard the sweet sound of familiarity and ran towards it, but peeked out the peep-hole for certainty.

[Trish] "Val, are you okay? It's Trish-I heard you yelling. V, answer me! Listen, I've called the police, so whoever you are, you're going to jail if you've hurt her."

Hearing sirens in the distance, Val opened just enough to pull Trish in.

[Val] "Oh gawd, Tri get in here!"

Val in full panic mode dragged Trish into the kitchen. Her once sun kissed dark skin was now as pale as the Cullen vampires in Twilight. Trish gasped.

[Trish] "Whaaaa the fucc Val. Damnnnn, how, why - oh lawd!" Trish pointed to the floor screaming. "Val, his brains are running." Trish covered her mouth and ran to the sink, slipping on a few obstacles but made it in time to vomit out everything inside of her. "Dammit V, you killed him and I've called the police! I thought someone was hurting you and well - now I."

Trish's voice faded as she backed up towards the wall. She wasn't afraid of Val but she was cautious. Val read Trish's expression and.started explaining.

[Val] "Tri, he was trying to kill me. I had no choice. What could I do? It was either him or me. I didn't know I'd hurt him this bad. I was only trying to get him off me. Do you see me? Look at meeeee! I didn't do this to myself! He did this to me!"

Trish looked at her friend's face which didn't look like anything was wrong. Her skin was now perfect, the cuts and bruises were no more. She wasn't even swollen. Val ran to the mirror to see the damage, but shook her head in disbelief. She couldn't explain what was going on, but she knew what she'd just experienced. Her words were as broken as her spirit as she cried inconsolably. Trish quickly ran to her and went to work making moves as if Olivia

Pope's team was in her ear. Val looked on curiously.

[Trish] "Did you tell him V? -Val stood dazed and confused. Trish snapped her fingers- Earth to you, Val. Did you tell him?"

Val shook her head no. The police were at the door banging-threatening to kick it in. Trish cocked her hand back and punched Val square in the eye causing her to hit the floor. The glass went through her skin easily and blood was all over her. Trish was pleased..

[Trish] Sorry sis, let me handle this please. I gotchu."

It wasn't as if Val had a choice since she was knocked the fuck out. Trish ran to the door and opened wide, instructing the police to follow her. They stood over the bodies lying on the floor. Tears filled Trish's eyes as she began shaking Val's arm violently. The policeman urged her to quit touching the bodies.

[Trish] "Val, are you alive? It's your neighbor. Can you hear me?"

The two male officers, one Black the other Hispanic, seemed edgy. Trish was grateful for having learned a thing or two from Val on how to seduce without suspicion and this time was the perfect opportunity. The Hispanic officer pulled his gun pointing at Trish. Completely unruffled, Trish outstretched her arms and gestured to the officer to lower his weapon. She licked her lips and rubbed her breast together perfectly. She wasn't big in size, but she was beautifully exotic to the eyes.

[Trish]"Forgive me, I have this habit of doing uncomfortable things when scared. This is my neighbor. I heard her screaming all the way in my home. I grabbed my gun called yall and ran over. I do have a license to carry officers. Anyways, I know where her spare key is, so I used it to get inside. Blood was everywhere. He's her ex-boyfriend. -She took a pregnant pause, pointed at Josh then inhaled deep as she rubbed her temples- Val told me they broke up days ago. Looks like he didn't take it well. Officers, I don't know if she's dead or not because I was attempting to check for life when you banged the door. "Val get up pleaassseee!" Ya think he choked her to death? There's blood everywhere. Please lower your weapons! Listen, I'm the one who made the call, not the one who committed the crime."

Trish was incontestable and next in line for an Oscar after that performance.

The police put their guns away and Val began coughing. She barely moved so the Black officer wrapped his arms around her waist and slowly lifted her to her feet. She looked down at Josh's body and fell limp into the officer. He consoled her a little more than he should've, but Val didn't mind. His energy comforted her. She welcomed it. Truth is, she needed to feel something more than karmic vibes.

Moments later the officer escorted Val out, still resting her head on his shoulders, holding tightly as she limped unhandcuffed into the backseat of his patrol car. Trish instructed she'd be there shortly then made the necessary calls as instructed. Moments after, Josh was being carried out in a body bag. Once he was placed into the van, Trish put up her middle finger and mumbled 'good riddance'. Shortly after that a black car sped off leaving tire marks on the street.

***

Chapter 2

Sisters and Secrets

Trish slammed the front door behind her and collapsed. The thought of any other scenario happening forced her small frame to trimmer with fear. She pressed her back against the tall vintage door and wrapped her arms around her knees. She turned from right to left and surveyed the room for damages. Blood splatters, shattered glass, torn oil paintings and Val's extravagant amethyst decorated the house. She thought of the kitchen, knowing there's much to do, and sighed deeply. She dropped her face in her hands and deeply inhaled. She repeated her breathing trying desperately to relax and hype herself to clean the mess. **[Trish]** "Look at me focused deep breathing and shit. I would've never done this without Val's crazy ass! Oh God she didn't deserve this! "

She daydreamed of her and Val's connection.

Trish grew up in the system, but not entirely. Her mother, Ms. Sweets, was so career driven that Trish found it hard understanding how she found time to have sex, let alone babies. Her only focus was money and lots of it. It wasn't to maintain a certain image or lifestyle, but more of a way to create a new life; one that excluded Trish and her older brother Percy. It wasn't odd she didn't know either of their dads because she really didn't know either of her children. When Trish was around 7 years of age her mother had enough and gave Trish away to her grandmother. Percy wasn't with her for the transaction, so she figured he was still with their mother, but she doubted that. He was probably living on the streets since he was 7 years her senior. Trish's grandmother Millie Ann wanted nothing to do with her, so she threatened Trish with release into the system and grandmother made good on her promise.

Because of her short stature Trish was teased and bullied for many years and did nothing but bawl up, cry and pray one day her brother would come save her. She gave up on that idea after her grandmother's passing and 7 years of silence. As the years dragged by she grew tired of being afraid and bullied and like a firecracker, she popped off and shook up the room. She didn't fight like the average girl- she was baby Mike Tyson.-a gift she didn't see coming or how to control when it came.

At the age of 16 she left on a journey to find her brother, but all she found was judgment and pitfalls. Trish's presence was poor and easily looked over. Men disregarded her as lesbian due to her warobe of baggy clothes and unkept hair. Women constantly approached, but she wasn't impressed or inspired to try anything. She was a virgin and destined to stay that way until meeting Val.

Trish never wanted to let on she was homeless because Val was always so polite with a smile or greeting whenever she saw her walking. Val would always extend an invite for coffee and Trish would always decline. Georgia's temperatures were unpredictable and this fall day was pretty cool. Like usual, Val invited her in for coffee and Trish was hesitant, but Val's gregarious manner made Trish open up. All night they talked and talked, forming an instant bond. Trish even opened up about being homeless and Val allowed her to stay the night. From that day they became a family doing everything together, including all of Val's DIY projects. Val, being an only child, appreciated having what she called a 'sister friend' and Trish couldn't have been happier.

Trish didn't grow up with religion of any kind so it took a while to get fully on board with all the natural and majestic things Val introduced. However, once she saw the instant gratifications, she was hooked. Her confidence and beauty shot through the roof. Her face became an exotic beauty to behold of golden-brown hues, high cheekbones, slanted eyes, and a mole under her bottom lip. The same men that overlooked her are the same men who stop and stare. Her smile was full of pearly whites, some of the bottom row was a little crooked, but still a beautiful smile. Her breast- nice and firm B cup- but her booty brought everything into a BIG perspective. She stood only 4'11, but her attitude and ass was gigantic. Her once wild untamed hair was now cut into a cute pink mohawk with tapered sides and one long purple loc hanging in the back just so Val would hush about her hairstyle. She couldn't deny her life improved by the thousands meeting Val so there was no way she'd allow Josh or anyone to ruin their sisterhood and only family.

Boom Boom Boom!!! The knock startled Trish. Quickly jumping to her feet, she looked through the peephole Val heighted for her. People dressed in black with large bags crossing their chest stood on the stairs looking focused and impatient. She assumed the man in charge was the one obstructing her full view of everything and everyone.

[Trish] "Yes, who are you?"

[Man] "Hi Trish, I'm here for Val. She called me from the police station letting me know what transpired here today. I am only here to take care of that. Will you open the door please Trish?" She didn't respond.

[Man] "I understand this seems a bit odd. Trust me, I know but I am here for a good reason. Val knew you couldn't do it. Hey, she will explain it all once you pick her up from the station." He assured her.

[Trish] "So how do you know Val?"

Trish cracked the door and looked up at his tall frame. He winked. She relaxed and opened the door a little more. She wasn't afraid of any false moves because her gun was still on her side.

[Trish] "Excuse me, but who are you? How do you know Val?" She looked him up and down with a defying glaze. "I know everyone she knows except you and that's pretty odd to me."

[Man] "I understand this Trish, but who I am is of no importance-

why I am is. I came strictly to do a job for my friend who happens to know your friend Val. I've been, well – he turned his body and pointed to the crew- we've been doing this for years. There's nothing we haven't seen and kept to ourselves. Understand?"

Trish shook her head of understanding and allowed him entry. He smiled and thanked her then waved everyone else in. Turns out the big bags held all the supplies and everything else needed. They immediately went into cleaning mode.

[**Man]** "We're only here to make things as normal as possible before she returns. It is our duty and honor seriously. Now, I'm afraid I can't say much more, but I can say it's nice meeting you- besides pretty lady - you've seen all of us. You can easily describe and point us out in a line up." He winked again, she blushed feeling safe and satisfied with his explanations then walked away.

[Trish] "I'm glad he's dead!"

Suddenly, the amethyst that was safely cradled on the floor shattered. Everyone froze and looked at each other. Trish grabbed her chest and pulled a piece of the hummingbird's beak pricking her skin. He walked fast towards her placing his hand on her shoulder.

[Man] "Trish are you alright? I don't know whaa – what just – it was just there right?"

He was confused but Trish understood well. She assured everyone she was okay and that it was only a scratch. Truth is she was shaking and couldn't wait to tell Val what happened. She hopped in her car and sped off to get her sister-friend.

***

Chapter 3

Promises and Plans

October -2017

He threw his shirt across the one green reclining chair sitting in his big living room. That was the only big space in the two-bedroom condo. The room reeked of stale smoke and molded clothes which matched the decor perfectly. He hadn't moved for a month until this day. This day was his only reason to survive the brokenness of his heart. He walked over to the stainless-steel refrigerator, stained by old food and dried seasonings, and grabbed a red stripe beer. Without looking he pulled out the crooked wooden drawer, felt around, popped his beer then fell into the recliner.

[Rage] "I'mma kill haa! Val killed em' and don't think she gotta pay for dat shit? Dees mufuckas talkin bout self-defense. For black folk, the justice system izza fucking joke. I shoulda killed ha ass in da courtroom. Dey got huh sounding like Mutha Theresa, but I know dat bihh Medusa. Dey cuhvern up for dat psycho bih, but cho days numbered hoe and I'm counting faster den my mind can think. I hate chu biiiihhh!!"

His voice echoed through the empty house as he looked towards the sky speaking. He took several big gulps of his slightly cold beer then punched the air.

[Rage] "Josh manee, you promised it'll only take a minute. I told cha take da gun bruhh!"

He leaped from the recliner dropping his remaining beer on the floor-it wasn't much left, but he didn't care either way. He removed his blazer, slinging it across the room then punched the beige wall until blood rolled down his wrist and twisted around his arms like bracelets. Pure exhaustion and exposed knuckles sent him falling in a position of prayer. The pain surged through his body like half of his soul was being ripped. He tried using his hands to lift his body off the floor but instead fell hard on his face. He laid there, face down ass up and feeling as empty as his asshole before finding strength to roll over on his back holding his hands where he could see them. He saw swelling and white bones protruding where his dark brown knuckles once were. He closed his eyes and began swearing.

[Rage] "This funky hoe Val -the dead one- gone pay -shiiiid a life foe a life. Stupid bastards ruled fuccin self-defense! Sed yu juz annuda black mane dey on't hafta kill; dats some cruel shit."

Tears rolled into his ears as mucus choked his next words. Sweat began pouring down his brows leaving his eyes burning.

"Fuccin judge and jury paying for dis too! I took pictures of all dey funky azz! Dey'll meet cha in da grave."

He walked past Josh's room as usual, but nothing about today was usual. He doubled back and kicked open the door. Josh had a slight case of OCD with the need to have things in perfect order, so the room was as he left it, nice and neat with just a queen sized bed, dresser and nightstand.He knocked down everything in his path including the pictures of them from their last vacation that proudly sat on the nightstand. With one kick, the top of the black nightstand detached and went flying to the other side of the room crashing before falling on the juice stained dingy carpet. He opened the closet and calmly brushed through Josh's shirts with his blood stained hands. He packed the shirts and other desired items into a small suitcase and placed them onto the square island separating the kitchen and living room. The rest of the items were laid neatly across Josh's bed. He looked around the room, seeing everything where it needed to be, then walked over to the dresser, grabbed the pictures and threw it with all his might into the mirror. The glass went crashing as the dresser flipped over. He stomped the dresser until his foot went through to the other side. Blood was now dripping from his hands and leg all over the carpet. Fragments of the nightstand were thrown into the dresser knocking the Family Dollar paintings from the walls into his pile of pity. This went on for a half hour before he flopped down on the bed. He laid on his back and stared at the stippled ceiling before closing his eyes. He heard a knock on the door and instantly sat up. He figured his nosey ass neighbor was telling him he's too loud and today was the perfect day to ensure his neighbor would regret complaining. The knock was rhythmless and rapid and this inflamed him. He opened the door with swiftness.

[Rage] "Yeah, wut da fucc yu want?"

Minutes turned to moments and those moments turned to hours before his company left. He smiled then walked towards Josh's room to get some sleep since it was the only place that held some form of living. Having his hands now perfectly wrapped and two strong painkillers flowing through his blood, he pushed the unwanted shirts into his pity pile when a cell phone rolled to his feet. He popped another Oxycodine then charged the phone. Once the phone had juice it displayed 7 unread messages. He lit his blunt -opened the first message- then inhaled. His jaw dropped as he went through the messages and pictures. He wrote down some numbers then threw the phone against the wall breaking its contents.

[Rage] "Sneaky bihhh bouta catch more den deez hands! I know what da fucc ta do nii! Dis bouta be a breeezeee!!!"

***

Chapter 4

Watching and Waiting

2 YEARS LATER - September 2019

The cool of the day was perfect for a drive so Val packed up everything and headed for Trish's.

[Val] "Trish, can you watch her for a little while? I've got to run to the grocery store and grab some items for the dinner party tonight. You're still coming right?"

Val looked forlorn as Trish laughed at her unraveling.

[Trish] "Yes, girl I told you imma be there. You are so on edge. (Trish chuckled) Calm yo ass down. It ain't like you're entertaining people you don't know. It's just me, your parents, your new-but not so new- maynee and did I mention grand ole ME hunty! Girl, take a deep breath, exhale and go on sumwhur. I will handle babygirl."

Val looked on shockingly as Trish extended her arms and the baby leaped into them.

[Val] "What have you done to my baby? She's never reacted that way. She's leaping into your arms neglecting my embrace. Now explain this little ms lady!" -Val laughed as she lightly squeezed her daughter's cheeks. – "Don't let aunty make you forget your mommy! I birthed and bathed you -she just spoils you with sugar and spice and that's not all that nice."

Trish desired to have everything in its perfect place and Val knew moving anything would cause Trish's anxiety to shoot through the roof. So when Trish teased Val and pushed her into the couch- she fell over in animated fashion- taking a few cushions with her landing softly onto the tan carpeted floor.

[Val] "See I told you Light-she's not so nice!"

Trish wouldn't allow Val to outdo her with the theatrics, so she flopped as well making it seem as if Val pulled her down. The baby screamed with delight as they played.

[Ora] "Again paaalease!"

Laughter ensued as Val assured her they'd play later. She waited until the baby ran off towards her play area before talking with Trish. She turned towards Val and threw a pillow at her face.

[Trish] "Val, stop messing up my place and get cho ass to the store girl. Time's a wastin!"

She tapped her wrist as if she were wearing a watch. Val pushed the pillow away then got up and started straightening her mess. She was procrastinating and Trish picked up on her energy.

[Trish] "What's wrong sis? I see you've placed your crown in your pocket. I don't see royalty ON or IN you at this moment. Talk lady!"

Val remained silent pretending to fluff the already plush cushions. Trish walked over and grabbed her hands. Val pulled away and grabbed Trish's face sweetly.

[Val] "All is well tiny tot!"

[Trish] "V, don't play with me!" She moved Val's hands away and stepped back, "What's up…I'm listening,"

She flipped out her ears like Dumbo.

[Val] "Girl yo ass looking like Martin Lawrence mixed with Will Smith! No seriously everything is fine. I'm just a little nervous about my parents meeting him. You know how they are, well you know how mom is." They laughed- "I just want everything to go right. It's been a minute since I've introduced them to someone."

Val turned towards her daughter. "She loves him T. I just want everything to be perfect."

[Trish] "Perfect? Girl no you didn't use perfect in the same sentence with people, places and things. Any and everything can and *will* always happen. There's no such thing as perfection, but there's such a thing as creating moments that will be perfect."

Val smiled in agreement. She picked up her purse, grabbed her keys, walked to the front door then pulled the handle opening it slightly.

[Val] "I know T. I'm just tripping because---"

Val's voice trailed off.

[Trish] "Val is something wrong? Did you drop something?"

Val didn't respond. She tilted her head then blinked her eyes. It was happening again and she didn't need anyone seeing anything she couldn't discuss. Trish opened the door wider to see what had taken Val's speech, but nothing was there. Val slightly smiled.

[Val] "No! Everything is fine. I thought I saw or felt something, that's all. It's nothing, I guess. The winds are changing T. There's a full moon tonight and it's the 13th to match this Friday."

She hugged Trish then did a little hop down the stairs before bouncing to her car.

[Trish] "See you later sissy!"

***

Chapter 5

Victory and Visions

Val sat back in her wine colored hatchback Mini Cooper and set her GPS for the nearest Aldi grocery store. She turned her music to a volume loud enough to be heard and tune others out. She hit a button and the windows rolled down. The wind felt good running through her locs like fingers. She bobbed her head and tooted her lips to a foreign language song with a dope beat. The thought of her daughter adapting easily to Aunty Trish made her smile from her heart.

[Val] "I can see it now. I get more time for yoga, meditation, and ME, yes me time!"

She popped her lips and allowed her free hand to dance with the wind. The aroma of the air was sweet like God was baking her favorite caramel pound cake. She took a big whiff and started chewing like she could taste it.

[Val] "Yes, Spirit, it smells and tastes delicious."

She laughed at herself and allowed her mind to drift. Her peacock trinket began blowing as if it were belly dancing. Crasssshhh! A bug committed suicide on her window diverting her thoughts. She wondered what made the bug risk it all, then turned on her wipers and rinsed its remains.

[Val] "Why bug? What troubles did you have sir -or umm -madame? I just washed this car. Why end it all and make things dirty?"

The air shifted stale as overwhelming thoughts of this very day two years ago rushed her mind. She shook her head back and forth as if thoughts from her brain would fall out of her ears. She secretly blamed Trish but would never admit it. Their argument of that day replayed in her mind. She remembered telling Trish it should stay her secret but Trish was convinced Josh had a right to know. Because she listened, things went from sugar to shit. Val rolled her eyes and a wet leaf intertwined within her fingers as the wind carried it across her face.

[Val]: "Ewwww, it's wet!"

She pulled it away and looked in the rearview mirror to check for remains and saw his face. His raging eyes, his frightening stare -even his unique scent of hatred and envy -glared back at her. Skrrrggh! The car swerved as horns honked jarring her back into the present moment. She pulled over to the emergency lane and gathered herself just enough to peel in traffic and exit at Pleasant Hill. She refused to look in the mirror until she was safely parked. She whipped into Aldi's parking lot- shut down everything- and just sat there. She slowly looked into the mirror. She prayed to see what she saw-just her sunflower colored eyes staring back at her. Relieved, she unzipped her purse and retouched her lip gloss.

[Val] "Dayuuumm, I can't believe his brains were all over my legs and face."

She shrugged at the thought then spoke with the winds hoping it'll reach Josh's ears.

[Val] "How did we get here? Your energy didn't match mine, but I was willing to help you get to a place of matching someone. Honestly, I didn't see a future or present with you- and to think we got a baby girl that you almost killed-you asshole! Unlike you, she's beautiful, smart, and MY Ora Unique Joy. She's my Light in all the darkness you tried creating. But you don't even deserve to know this!"

Her next words choked her up before dropping her head in her hands, sniveling..

“I was trying to tell you, but you didn’t give me a chance. Damn, I’ve murdered you, but you left me no choice. You smacked me, kneed me, spit on me. Fuck you Josh, fuck you!”

Val’s breathing became frantic as she heard her name clanging like tambourines in the wind. She lowered her seat to hide from watchful eyes and cried out.

[**Val**] “I tried. I really did. What was I thinking? What was he thinking? Why couldn’t he just allow me to explain? It went too far. Josh, it went too far!”

She punched the steering wheel and held her hand there before overhearing someone walking by asking if she was alright or crazy. She glared at the nosey couple, never breaking eye contact until they walked in the store.

A strong breeze rocked her car and she understood her pity party was over. She closed her eyes and silently affirmed. *‘Today I celebrate my new life, new love and new energy. Thank you Spirit, ancestors, angels and guides for always keeping me in the now of life. I am forever grateful’* She blew kisses to the wind then untwisted her jasper and black tourmaline crystal necklace, licked her tongue across her teeth, did a quick breath check, then opened the door. A loud crash came from the hood. Her body froze, but her eyes scoped the scene, yet nothing or no one was there.

She opened the car door slowly before getting out of the car.

***

Chapter 6

Munchie and Memories

[Trish] "I can't believe you jumped in my arms like that! Look at you! You're growing so fast Ora- my lil Munchie."

She pinched her cheeks then placed her on the floor and like any other kid, Ora took off running. Trish allowed her to run without worry because her house became baby proof once she found out Val was pregnant. She wasn't extremely happy about the father, but she beamed with pride anyway especially when Val honored her as godmother. She was grateful Ora looked nothing like her father but she knew Val was more grateful.

Ora was a perfect brown color of the finest chocolate with yellow hues. Her afro was big, sandy red and full of thick curls. Her little plump lips housed her 4 maxillary and 4 mandibular incisors. Her hazel green eyes were almond shaped and bright. She was super smart, full of personality and was fully potty trained before her 1st birthday.

[Trish] " Ora Munchie, where are you at? You're too quiet. I know you're doing something you shouldn't."

Munchie ran from the kitchen laughing with her cheeks fuller than usual.

[Trish] "Girl come here. What's in your mouth?"

Trish held out her hand but she refused to give up the goods. Trish went in fast, tickling her belly causing her to spit everywhere, but mainly Trish's hand.

[Ora] "Ew, naztee!"

Trish picked saliva filled chips from her hair, shirt and face. She scrunched her nose in disapproval.

[Trish] "It's your nasty luh girl. You put all this spit in my hands. I should rub it on you, but I see what's going on hurr. You're restless aren't cha? You always eat junk food when you're bored. Mommy must've had you up all day chanting huh!" -Trish chuckled at the thought. -"C'mon little lady!"

Ora popped her lips just like Val then followed Trish around like a lost puppy. When Trish made a sudden stop, she ran into her leg and fell over in laughter. Sometimes she would fall on purpose just so she could get picked up. Trish began bouncing Ora up and down as she walked towards her rocking chair. She couldn't resist the motion and calmness of rocking and would fall asleep within minutes. She looked at Trish as if she knew what was going on and kicked her feet like she was running on air. She shook her head no and tried squirming, but Trish held her tighter. She lit her lavender scented candle and waited patiently for Ora to inhale the fumes. Her breathing calmed and Trish began slowly rocking and singing.

[Trish] *"Lil Munchie, my bookie, my tiny little bunny. You're sleepy, eyes heavy, now you can start dreaming hunty."*

Ora fell silent as if she was under the greatest hypnosis. Trish remembered how Val would throw parties just to hear her sing then compare her voice to an angel. Ora must've agreed because within minutes she was snoring. Still rocking, she eased up out of the chair and quietly laid her on the couch. Walking into the kitchen, her favorite room in the house, she smiled. She was grateful with appreciation of her kitchen's décor of reds and dark blues throughout her med size room. She loved the window placement above the sink allowing her plants to have light and fresh air. She opened the window, inhaled the aroma of the wind, and smiled as the scent of fresh pine hit her nose. She couldn't believe she allowed Val to talk her into planting pine trees, but she was grateful she did. The smell was amazing and the given calm was relaxing. She finger traced her purple succulent as she walked towards her dishwasher to put away dishes.

Woolgathering thoughts of Val played in her head. She knew why Val was distracted, but she figured if she didn't say anything then it wouldn't be anything. She took a deep breath and blew it out. She grabbed her cell phone and pulled up YouTube. She needed to hear some music as she prepared for Val's dinner party. Ari Lennox popped up and Chicago Boy blared just loud enough for Trish to kick it without waking the baby. She grabbed a plate, wiped it dry and began dancing and daydreaming. -

[Trish] "Things just went too far. I had to protect her. She didn't need jail, especially being with a child. I couldn't allow that. Things just went - I should have just -NO Trish, no... no...no. I could have killed him with my bare hands if he'd hurt her. I won't allow anyone to hurt either of them. They are my only friends and family. I'd die if ---NO Trish-stop thinking this way!"

She began beating the sides of her head.

[Trish] "Change the thoughts- I have the power. My thoughts don't control me, I controllll—Ya know what- he deserved everything he got. He barged into her space and demanded whaaat exactly? How dare he say he loves her one day and try to kill her the next? That's crazy. I will stay single forever before I deal with that type of headache or heartbreak. Puhlease, I don't need that type of energy in my life. They can have all that. Saaang Ari with your chocolate self!! Sannnng bitchhhhh! Ya know what-I'm glad he's dead. You whack son of a – well, I don't know yo momma, so I won't disrespect her, but fuck you with long broomsticks! Oooh umm change the thoughts. I have the power to change myyyy"-

BAAM! A plate fell, snapping into pieces and cutting across the top of her foot. She welcomed the pain with a deep inhale then slowly exhaled with relief. She grabbed a paper towel and began wiping the blood. She picked up the plate and threw its remains in the trash. She began humming as she looked out her kitchen window enjoying nature. She felt a strange presence and quickly turned around. She checked on Ora -who was still sleeping peacefully- then walked back in the kitchen. Again, she went to the window and allowed the breeze to comfort her nostrils and embrace her body.

“Fuck you too.” A voice whispered.

Trish jumped looking around, completely turning in a circle. She didn’t see anyone, but she couldn’t deny the presence felt. She heard laughter and realized children were playing right up under her window. She shook her head in relief and kept humming.

***

Chapter 7

Anger and Admiration

Rage gave himself a once over in the mirror admiring his all black everything except his button up turquoise shirt that complimented his light brown skin. Internally he thanked the clerk for pointing it out. He grabbed his CBD beard oil and began rubbing his face. He sprayed his 'Straight to Heaven' cologne by Kilian and adjusted his black rimmed glasses. He closed the cabinet door and stared at himself in the mirror.

[Rage] "Dey gone die wen dey see meh!" He did a breath check then grabbed a green tic tac. "I'm killing dees hoes in dis right hurr, literally!"

He began imitating Michael Jackson's spin until laughter filled his entire body and dizziness filled his mind. He popped his collar wishing Josh could see him. He felt closest to Josh in his old room so he walked in admiring the remodeling he'd done.He wanted and needed to talk with him. He'd gotten rid of everything but the bed and one sweater he kept hanging neatly in the closet. It was the only sweater that carried Josh's smell throughout the room. Tonight was the night- the night of all nights-the night Josh would finally rest in peace. He began singing Betty Wright's hit song with some adlibs of his own.

[Rage] "*Wooohooo! Tonight is da nite I kill a bih! I sed I won't be gentle* *withchu- I promise I won't. I'm shaking, I'm trembling- waiting on yu ta walk in!"*

He danced around with his swisher blunt stuffed with loud kush. With every inhale he switched characters. This time he was Denzel Washington in 'Training Day'.

"I'm puttin cases on all you bishes."

He held the blunt between his fingers then blew smoke in the air gesturing for Josh to take a shotgun before falling into the recliner throwing one leg over the armrest.

[**Rage**] "Aye Josh, lemme tell ya dis bih wasted no time movin on. She gotta damn babey bruh. She bouta be an orphan doh- ya feel me! His laugh was condescending. "Ya right, bruh dat's harsh, but fucc it and fucc em'.. I tell ya wut, I'mma send em' bouf ta ya. I sure as hell know killing dem means I die, so we all gone party in hell."

His phone chirped. He read the text and stood up. ` ` Aye bruh, dees hoes want me mannne! The streets talm bout I look like yung Mike Epps, but we know I look way betta! I stay on a mission. Speaking of missions, I'm out! Next time we talk shit'll be diff fam."

He gave himself another look in the mirror before hopping in his black Cobalt speeding off into the night.

***

Chapter 8

Wine and Worry

[Val] "Trish, hurry up. They're going to be here in a minute. You know everything gotta be perfect and you look amazing by the way!"

She opened the large double French doors in the kitchen urging Trish to come in. Val snapped her fingers each time Trish switched her hips, rocking her beautiful ensemble of denim and diamonds. Her 4'11 height was now an easy 5'2 with the thigh high heeled boots.

[Val] "Well don't you look expensive!"

Trish smiled and playfully slapped Val's hand away. She put Ora down and she took off running to her play area in the kitchen. She had a playroom in every room except bedrooms, understanding that playtime was over whenever she entered that room.

Trish looked around the house-

[Trish] "I know our mom V, she's definitely going to pick this house, as beautiful as it is, and you apart. -She poked Val's arm teasingly- "So I'm doing my part to make sure things are just as she likes it, which is having ME in it!"

[Val] "Girl you are a mess, but seriously I don't know what I'd do without you. You're forever there for me."

Val gave Trish a look of gratitude and they embraced. She fingered through Trish's tight curls as always and Trish pushed her hand away as usual. Val smiled and then went to check on her baby girl while Trish busied herself with things Val may have overlooked. Secretly, she desired things to be just as perfect as Val desired, but she'd never tell her.

She stood in the kitchen admiring the work of the dining area. Val loved exquisite and unique things, so it was no brainer when Trish saw the Orren Ellis inspired DIY extendable dining table dressed in beautiful blue orchid phalaenopsis arrangements. Everything was neatly placed, even the rainbow aura quartz crystal strategically latched in the table's design.

Val returned with a shove to Trish's back.

[Val] "Girl where did you get the name Munchie from anyways? Why can't you get with the program and call her Light as I do?"

Trish turned to face Val.

[Trish] "It's because she eats all the time -like she dun smoked 5 blunts or sumthin. It's always veggies- and they're always half eaten. And what almost 2-year-old child wants chickpeas -now, that's not a bad thing but whose 2 yr old wants it? You know I only buy that nasty mess because my baby loves it. What you over here feeding this child anyway?"

Before Val could answer, Trish thought of something.

[Trish] "Oh, my goodness girl, listen I had sum Red Hot Riplets around the house and she got into em. Then spit em in my hands talm bout naztee eww! Girl, I almost lost it. You know how I feel bout my Old Vienna St. Louis best everrr chips. She's completely disruh-spectful!"

Val burst into laughter knowing things were serious whenever Trish talks with all the R's. She changed the subject then tapped Trish on the shoulder. They sat down at the marble double stacked island. Trish adjusted her seat and watched Val perplexingly.

[Val] "Tri you know today marks 2 years since the incident. I hadn't thought about it since that night, but today I saw his face in the wind. I smelled his stench. I saw his brains all over my legs and face." -Val put her hand under her chin as if she were posing for a picture- "One thing that always bothered me was how he knew about Jay. He had a fucking picture of us meeting for the first time, us talking at the park and us kissing at dinner. Was he stalking me?"

Trish looked on with a blank expression. Val waved her off and kept talking.

[**Val**] "He broke up with me dammit-so it's weird he'd stalk. Tiny tot this is a great night for me right. I'm not going to spend another moment thinking about him!"

[**Trish**] "Oh my god Valerieeeee Sky Joy, calm down. This is not the night to revisit the days of old loves and hard lessons. We must stay in the present moment.You hear me talking in Andrea Queen Joy's voice? That lets you know this thang is serious." -Laughter ensued-. "Besides, the bad worked for good. You just never know, Jay did suggest meeting your family and I like him for you Valerieeeee! By the way, you look stunning in your yellow sundress and those shoooes girl. Very magical indeed!"

Trish snapped her fingers twice and poked her lips.

[**Val**] "I know yo ass didn't just say my and my mother's government name in duplicates? You ain't slick Tri!! You know momma ain't been Andrea since her Baptist days. She is Queen now. The one and only!"

Val took a bow and Trish saluted before laughing.

"Don't be calling me no damn Valerie. I hear it enough at work. I swear I want to change it and someday I will. I'm thinking something that says love since my baby is Light. Whatcha think about Ahava?"

[**Trish**] "I don't!"

Val jerked her head back and frowned her lips. Seconds later she reacted as if she were hit with a bolt of lightning and began jumping up and down. She ran to Trish and interlocked their fingers, forcing her to jump in excitement also. Trish liked this energy better.

[Val] "Wop wop....so, girl you think he gone ask me?"

[Trish] "Oh my gawwwd V, you never know. I mean he loves you and you love him right, so why not? I don't even get to see you as much cuz you always cuffed with his ass, so it's like you're married anyway!"

Val mushed Trish as they shared a laugh before busying themselves with the rest of the cooking.

[Trish] "Valerie, I'm going to run this trash out back."

Val gasped at the nerve of Trish then splashed water in her face.

[Trish] "Stop, okay, okay. I won't use the name again tonight. Now, do you have any more trash I should grab?"

[Val] "Ummm, no I think I cleaned out the trash from the upstairs bathrooms, my room, the guest room and baby girl's room. I think I got it all."

[Trish] "You said every room but my room. You left my room trashy?" She whined.

[Val] "Girl yo room is in yo house and yes I got it from the special room you deem as yours. – I can't believe you're still living over there. I couldn't stay in that house another day. Besides, I- Nope, enough of that. How's the new neighbors?"

Trish began placing the smaller bags of trash into the larger bag while twerking to her underground discovery of Oren Major. His '*Supergirl*' song blasted from her phone's speaker. In unison they sang '*Superman I'm just looking for a super chick- she working out and eating good she got super thick. I been working on these abs tryna get a six*!' Trish began backing it up and they laughed again which was all they seemed to do. Val was happy whenever Trish was around. She helped her get through the nights of uneasiness and nightmares. She'd become the nanny, the friend and lover in some sort. Val remembered waking up from one of her many imprisoning dreams and Trish spooning her into comfort. It didn't feel weird but appreciated. Neither had been with the same sex nor interested in changing the narrative of their relationship. Trish's job was doing whatever to see to it that Val returned to her peace and Val was desperate to get there.

[Trish] "Val, you know you want all of this peace and harmony. Look at this prize right here!" They laughed. "I assume the neighbor is cool. The only time I see her is when her fuck buddy comes over. He makes sure I see him every time. His music is always blasting in his lil black car. He's a cutie, but something about him is off to me V. He gives me the heebeegeebees vibes."

[Val] "Huh?! she chuckled. He cute though! T you sumthin else, but not the heebeegeebee vibes- well you already know how I feel about all that. You have to trust those instincts, or as I call it, insights."

[Trish] "I know girl! I keep my distance, but it's like he wants me to see him or something. Then, when I do acknowledge him he laughs like a school kid. Da ninja is weird man and talkin bout him makes me feel like I'm saying Candyman."

Val spit her drink as she laughed. Trish almost hit the floor dodging Val's outward display of humor.

[Val] "T, maybe he has a crush on you but gotta keep it cute for his girl, yo neighbor. You did say he was cute."

[Trish] "Girl bye!"

She was over it and the conversation. She laughed as she opened the French doors exiting through the patio entering the backyard. Val's backyard was immaculate and pretty much emulated her old yard minus a few pine trees. She had a huge elephant fountain surrounded by stones and rocks uniquely painted by her. Exotic succulents of all shapes, sizes and colors traced her stone walkway leading to her side door to prevent walking on her ground art.

[Trish] "I always feel like I'm a damn Avatar in this yard! Now why she paint her dumpster red and label caution on it? Lawwwd who dis woman!" She chuckled at the thought.

Having an eerie feeling she was being watched, she paused to look around. She didn't see anyone or anything, tossed the trash over and ran.

The side door was open, so she entered quietly. The smell of garlic, onions and fresh cilantro filled the air. Val was in a moment of her element and began burning sage, singing and aligning crystals throughout the house. Val entered her godliness and Trish loved it, realizing Val's connection and magic grew stronger as she stayed stagnant. She made a mental note to talk to Val about why.

[Trish] "Hey Val, come sage me down. I just had this strange feeling I was being watched. I mean I really feel eerie right now."

Val froze for a moment as she too had the same feeling earlier. She walked over to Trish without exchanging a word and began praying over her sister-friend. Trish began crying imploringly.

[Val] "T, what is wrong? Why are you crying?"

Val moved Trish's bangs to the side of her face. Trish was about to say something, but the doorbell rang. Val immediately walked towards the door.

[Trish] "I'm saved by the bell!"

[Val] "T don't think too quickly. We're revisiting this. That bell ain't save you. It just delayed this convo for continuation when we're alone."

Trish dashed off into the bathroom to fix her falling mink lashes and running mascara. She looked in the mirror and admired what she saw.

[Trish] "Look at me, the girly girl keeping my lashes thick and long with my nails and feet painted to perfeKkkchunnn. Who woulda thunk it! Certainly not me, but here I am- all fine and shit and I get the D when I desire." She spun her one purple loc round and round while fingering through her complementing dark pink mohawk. She refreshed her make-up, popped her lips and walked out ready.

[Trish] "Mom, are you fussing? I was in the bathroom for 5 seconds and I'm sure you've found fault in 20 different things"

Trish laughed as she and The Joy's embraced each other. Val escorted everyone down the hallway to the dining area. Her parents ahh/ooh quickly became oowww and awww's at the decor. They complimented everything and Val lit up like a Christmas tree. Pleasantries with the Joys were short lived, so she embraced the moment.

The Joys- regal, royal, and Blackity Black rich- were courteous and kind to all, but didn't tolerate nonsense. Always first to volunteer in helping others and last to leave another behind. Basically, they were people who other people respected and wished to replicate. It wasn't always this way, but when the tables turned, they turned in favor of JOY!

Mrs. Joy, birth name is Andrea Queen Niel, is known for saying what she means and meaning every word, no filters. She's a beautiful brown woman with locs of gray that brings out her cocoa brown hues perfectly. Let her tell it -the gray hair is her crown of wisdom- and she is very wise. It wasn't always this way, but ever since the tragic day of Victor, she became a victorious Queen. She never looked back on her baptist beginnings, but became forever known as Queen. She and Val could pass for twins if it weren't for Val being shorter. She's youthful in looks but well-seasoned when she speaks. You always know you're in the presence of a virtuous woman. She runs a business that supports, feeds, clothes and loves the homeless and hurting. They are guaranteed to receive any and everything from counseling, hands on training, to spiritual lessons, guided meditation, Reiki healing, chakra alignments and sometimes spell work. Basically, wherever the spirit leads, she obliges. Queen believes in the mantra of coming in one way and leaving another.

Mr. Tracy Lee Joy is the total opposite. He's a careful man. He keeps his words limited, speaking only when spoken too or when needed; so when he speaks everyone pays attention. He's tall in stature 6'3, coconut skin tone, giving off an aura and stare of that famous rapper Ice Cube with his eyes and intense facial expression, but friendly, funny and simple in adapting. His riches stem from a hunch of investments in many franchised cannabis farms in LA. He'd made a profit within 2 years and relocated her family to LA and started several businesses. He retired from the CEO spotlight - leaving it in the hands of his trusted partners – and relocated back to Atlanta, GA. His mother named him Tracy, but the streets named him King Joy. His wife only knows him as her Joy. He continued his wealth by purchasing a few vacant buildings and transforming them into a square block set of brownstones. Trish used to be a tenant but soon became the owner of hers after King Joy placed it in her name. They love Trish as their own and never wanted her to worry about being displaced again. With his monthly profits, King Joy gifted Val a treasured fixer upper for a fraction of the price. She converted her land into a beautiful mini mansion having 5 bedrooms with 5 ½ bathrooms. It may have been a drive to Trish, but she was away from the place that held her darkest secret. If King Joy's girls are happy, he's happy. Spoiling them like crazy was his happiness and he couldn't get enough. He even had a brownstone signed over for his grandbaby when she turned 18. If he had 99 problems money wouldn't be one.

[**Queen**] "So where is this new man? Is he an energy expert and freak like you? Do the ancestors accept him? I prayed, but things were silent."

[**Val**] "Momma!!"

Val grabbed her chest as if she was clutching invisible pearls. King Joy blushed, feeling his daughter's embarrassment he shook his head in disbelief of his wife's vulgarity. She didn't care about either of their feelings and waved them off.

[**Joy**] "Where's my grandbaby- my little Ora? I was telling your mom how I thought you were going overboard with this energy mess, but Ora's Hebrew meaning of 'light' brought me complete joy. Ha ha! See how I did that there, pun intended." He playfully pushed Val's shoulder and kept talking. "Anyways, where is she?"

The way his eyes began dancing as he looked around for Ora, was the way Val's heart danced whenever he was around. He was Val's rock, her strong tower, her best friend. She loved looking upon his face, standing on her toes to kiss his forehead and holding tightly to his words of wisdom. He reminded her of strength. He was her Obatula on earth and she'd always be daddy's little girl.

[**Val**] "Dad, Light's in her playroom probably sleeping. Aunty Trish musta wore her out"- Queen came around the corner bouncing Light on her hip- "Welp nevermind!"

[**Queen**] "I already got her Joy. Isn't she adorable? Granny's baby-girl."

Light was pulling on her granny's locs wrapping her fingers in two at a time. Joy went in for a kiss, but Queen pulled her away.

[Joy] "Can you stop hogging all her love? I wanna hold my grand-daughter!"

Light grabbed her granddad's face and kissed the tip of his nose leaving a little saliva bubble on it. He didn't care one way or the other. He smiled and jumped around into a spin. Light burst into laughter.

[**Ora**] "Again, again puhlease!"

She kicked her little feet in excitement. He was so tickled that he did it again and again. Each time she laughed harder than the last. Queen warned him to stop before he spun the sense out of his head or broke some weak bones. He didn't care. He was having the time of his life being surrounded by all the women he loved. Besides, she was his *light,* and everything was right in his world. Gran-dad grew tired of spinning, so he used what he knew to get Light away from her grandmother. He walked over to Trish and started dancing. Light wiggled her way down and ran over and pushed Trish away. He was hers only. Everyone began laughing. King Joy swooped up Light and danced like it was just the two of them in the room.

***

Chapter 9

Soulmates and Stalkers

Jay was dressed in his usual fitted slacks, button up, and stoned jewelry accessories. His style was sleek-sexy and seductive. He looked festive in his canary yellow and diamond shoes. Val smiled knowing they didn't plan being in sync but it never failed. Jay Adefeso Ogun, known as Jay O to his close friends stood 6'5, dark smooth skin with a thick salt and pepper beard. His eyes dazzled in hazel as his lips- nice full dark pink- and muscular build always made the ladies take notice. His hair was long and his loc's usually flowed to the tip of his butt, but tonight he wore a man bun. She always called him her tall hazel eyed Daniel Kaluuya-you know the black guy in 'Get Out', 'Black Panther' and a host of others. Him, yes him but on some sexy sexy. She noticed he trimmed his beard and went to reach for it, but he pulled her hand towards his heart causing his arm to play a tune as his bracelets of many stones, chakra, and charms touched. He didn't wear it for show but more of a statement, or extension of himself. He and Val were truly one of a kind. He smiled then handed her a bouquet of purple lilies, tulips, sunflowers and midnight blue orchids. It didn't make sense to the florist when he chose the arrangement, but he wasn't trying to make sense-he was trying to make a statement. She grabbed them and deeply inhaled enjoying the resinous scent and how delicious they'd look in her living room. It was perfect for Val.

[**Jay**] "Hey baby, sorry I'm late. There was an accident off 285 and Chamblee Tucker. Traffic was bumper to bumper for about 30 minutes. I was a half mile from your exit, but it took me half a year to get to it."

Val laughed as they held each other around the waist before exchanging a passionate kiss. She was careful not to linger, yet like clockwork, Queen began yelling.

[**Queen**] "Okay, get in here so we can see you. Y'all got all night to talk plus we're hungry. Don't you smell all this goodness?"

Hand in hand, Jay and Val walked into the dining room. Val took a deep breath ready for introduction, but Jay was quicker than she'd realized.

[**Jay**] "Well hello beautiful." Jay stepped back and did a double take. "Wow, you and your daughter look so much alike. This is what I have to look forward to. I am not mad at all."

Jay looked over at Val and winked. Queen blushed hard causing her cheeks to become rosy red as if she'd applied blush.. Jay grabbed Queen's hand and kissed it. Her eyes fluttered. King Joy stood up from the table and cleared his throat. Jay might've had inches over him, but Joy stood eye to eye. Val looked on in full admiration.

Light walked over and raised her arms. Jay swooped her up kissing her all over her face.

[**Jay**] "How's daddy Light doing? Are you shining for the world to see?"

Light laughed cheerfully and everyone joined just as joyfully except Joy. He cleared his throat with bass making sure to get Jay's attention.

[**Joy**] "Alright there youngin, you already got my Princesses under your spell, you ain't gone get my wife. She's spoken for!" He looked Jay up and down with a frown. Amused, Jay reached out for a bro hug and daddy Joy pulled him in exchanging hefty laughter and slaps on the back. Light made sure to hug both their necks as each man melted like butter under her soft touch. Jay and Joy were seated at the table. They immediately began conversing on everything from business to bonds like they were old pals making the air friendly, pleasant and productive. “So how did you meet?”

Without warning they said the same thing. They laughed at each other for a moment while telling the other to just tell the story. Val won.

[Val] “The music blared as I danced alone, eyes closed, hips swaying vibrations higher than ever. Y’all know how I do. He danced with a circle of women, yet simultaneously we turned towards each other locking eyes and hands before saying one word. He was drooling at the mouth and I was just like ‘ahh wateva!”

[Jay] “Oh is that what you said? Tell the truth-you know we body scanned one another like crazy.”

They laughed, but Joy didn’t find it funny. Val sat up in her seat and fixed her face.

[Val] “What caught my attention was the long Jade crystal hanging from his neck. It was like- in that moment I understood why I held his hands and felt so protected.”

She looked at Jay who now was eyeing her like she was the only person in the room. He always made her feel genuinely special and she never wanted it to end. He wasn’t just fine-he was all man and all god simultaneously! He was her demigod on earth and she was well pleased. He grabbed her hand and intertwined their fingers then turned towards Joy.

[Joy] “Mr. Joy, I must be honest. I was fixated on her. I mean she had the earrings, bracelet and waist beads-looking like a walking billboard needing alignment.” Val playfully pushed him. “It was at that moment I understood why I felt so protective of her. I was sitting there with so many questions rushing my mind. Things like, did the universe get it on point, point? And just like that she spoke saying you match my fly. She thought I didn’t hear her, and I pretended I didn't, so I just winked.” In unison Jay and Val said the same thing and everyone around the table looked at each other confused and vexed.

[Val] "My name is -we both said together – kinda like now. We talked together all night, finishing each other's sentences. Basically our sync and inseparable behavior started that day and has been ongoing. That night after the club we stayed together, shared a meal and went to the park in the same clothes we'd just danced in. It didn't matter to us-we just didn't want to be without each other. I felt comfortable yet compelled to tell him about my newfound news of pregnancy and his response blew me away. He vowed to never leave me alone at any moment in life. He even said he's about to be a dad. I thought it was just a joke but as we can see he made good on his promise!"

With all the oohhs and aahhs nobody noticed her smile faded as she cringed thinking of how just one-week later Josh's brain would spill into the cracks of her kitchen floor. Jay's forehead kiss brought her back to the present. He knew what she needed and had no problems meeting her needs. She leaned into him and rested until she felt better. Joy smiled and patted Jay's back.

Val and Trish served the meal of Truffle bay scallops with celery puree'- Rosemary lemon salmon, brown sugar carrots and flaky homemade buttermilk biscuits. Everyone ate greatly and multiple times. Somewhere in between the wine and laughter, Light fell asleep and was placed in her bedroom.

[Val] "I hope y'all saved room for dessert. I made my famous caramel pound cake."

Jay and Joy's face lit up like the world had finally discovered peace on earth. Jay stood up to stretch and rubbed his belly in delight.

[Jay] "Baby, I didn't know you were going to make that cake. Let me run to the bathroom real quick, I gotta empty the left side so I can make room for that cake."

Trish looked up and frowned, placing her phone face down on the table.

[Trish] "Ewwww Jay! That's TMI sir."

Laughter erupted from everywhere as Val stood.

[Val] "Would anyone like a refresher of wine while I'm getting the cake?"

Jay went to grab everyone's glasses, but Val motioned him to sit down and enjoy himself. He thought about it and figured this would be the perfect time for his plan to manifest. He sat back and held up his glass. The Joys held theirs as well. Trish happily declined. Val started walking towards the kitchen.

[Val] "I'll just bring the bottle with the cake because I'm not pouring anything or carrying all those glasses."

Trish and Jay made eye contact. She gave him two thumbs up. He cleared his throat and turned towards Mr. Joy once Val was out of ear shot.

[Jay] "Sir-"

[Joy] "Yes, what is it son? I told you, this here my woman. You got you a nice one right there. Quit coming for me and mine."

Jay let out a nervous laugh then cleared his throat. He took a deep breath then exhaled slowly.

[Jay] "I've loved your daughter since the first day I met her. She is so intriguing to me. She has a great head on her shoulders. She's independent yet still makes me feel like a man that's needed. I owe a great thank you to the both of you- of course and I am forever grateful"- Jay cleared his throat again while rubbing his hands together.- "So, I wanted to know if I could umm, could, umm, can I have your daughter's hand in marriage, I mean if that's okay with you two?"

Queen covered her mouth while Joy's stare became piercing. Jay shifted in his seat.

[Joy] "Are you serious? Trish, is he serious?" Trish nodded her head yes. Joy turned to Jay and for a long moment he stayed silent. Jay looked on perplexingly until Joy decided to talk- "Yes, son you have my permission, my blessings. I know that you're a good man.

I have a good feeling about you. As all these ladies would say- you have good energy. My grandbaby loves you- I can clearly see that- hell, Stevie Wonder could too. It will be my honor to call you son." Joy and Jay stood up to embrace. Queen looked at her husband in disbelief and dropped her hands.

[Queen] "Oh, now you wanna talk about energy!"

He ignored her and placed his hand on Jay's shoulder.

[Joy] "Do you give him your blessing?"

[Queen] "Oh, yes -yes, you have my blessings. I'm so happy!! I've been waiting for this day for her. I get to plan a wedding and prepare for a new grandbaby. You're such a fine young man. In fact, I see a younger Joy." Jay's face lit up like lights. "But, slow yo roll- Trish what you think? Is he good?"

Trish shook her head in approval. She was smiling just as hard as The Joys.

[Trish] "He already knows how I feel about it. They act like they're married anyway! I barely get to see my sister, but when I do, she's always happy, a healthy happiness too."

Jay exhaled a relieving sigh. Daddy Joy couldn't hold the excitement and called out.

[Joy] "Princess, what's taking you so long with the wine and cake. Now you know I'm trying to get yo momma tipsy and pregnant. Matter of fact we'll take our cake to go. You know once she's sleepy it's a wrap for the cuddle session. C'mon Princess, get in here!"

Trish got up from the table and walked into the kitchen to see what was taking Val so long. She looked around the kitchen, the bathroom, but still no Val. She looked at the back door and noticed it was cracked open. She immediately felt eeriness surrounding her and slowly opened the door peeking out her head-

[Trish] "Val, are you out here? Valerie, where are you at, we're waiting on you."

Trish slammed the door and backed into Jay. She screamed and swung. Jay grabbed her hands and spun her around.

[**Jay**] Woo woo! Trish calm down, it's just me. Where's Val?" –

Trish jerked away and ran into the bathroom then the dining room. Jay looked at her confusingly as she ran from room to room.

[**Trish**] "Is Val in here?"

They looked at Trish sideways.

[**Joy**] "We thought you went to get her."

[**Trish**] "I went into the kitchen, but she wasn't in there. I checked the bathroom too."

[Joy] "Maybe, she's upstairs with Ora. Did you check there?"

Jay yelled up the stairs –

[**Jay**] "Val, my chocolate sugah -come downstairs. We're waiting on you- bring Light because I have some news to share."

Moments passed and still no Val. Joy looked perplexed and Jay immediately took off running upstairs. Trish wasn't far behind.

[**Jay**] "Val's not up here."

[**Trish**] "Ora Munchie not up here either. We checked all the rooms. Where are they?"

Everyone looked at the half open back door then at each other.

***

Chapter 10

Confusion and Compliments

[Rage] "Wake up bih!" He grabbed his bottle of water and shook it over her head. "Ya thought yu wuz gone getaway widdit? Damn, juz wen ya thank life iz great- BOOM BIH- hurr I am."

He dropped the empty bottle on her head, lit his blunt and sat in the chair across from her. He inhaled slowly as he looked in admiration of her beauty.

[Rage] "I' ain't no yu wuz dis fine. Dayyyuummm-I see why dat ninja flipped da fucc out over ya! No worries doh- da only flipping dunn ta nite is bullets frem dis gun. I'mma kill yu and dis slopping azz bebay too."

He started laughing then coughing. She tried moving her legs, but screeched in pain, tried opening her eyes, yet saw darkness. There was slight movement and Val quickly realized her baby was with her. She grabbed Light and held her tightly to her chest. She opened her mouth then closed it without saying a word. She inhaled deeply then exhaled all the air from her lungs. She repeated the breathing just enough to understand this situation was serious.

Rage became agitated, then demanded she stop breathing before he started unloading his gun.

[Val] "Who are you and where are we? What happened to my family?"

***

Chapter 11

Bias and Bradley

[Officer1] "So, you went into the kitchen- saw the door slightly opened and that's when you discovered she- excuse me- they were missing? Am I quoting you correctly Mrs. Sweets?"

One of the two white officers looked up from his writing pad to meet eyes with Trish for agreement. He was average height yet displayed a huge attitude. Typical white male with blonde hair and brown eyes. The other officer was taller, thicker, tanner, and extremely sexy. He had an arrogance of cockiness and confidence in him, and Trish was intrigued.

[Trish] "It's just Ms. Sweets, I'm not married, and yes that is what happened."

A smile crept from the corner of his mouth as he hurried to drop his head either in shyness or fear of his partner seeing.

[Jay] "Hi, I'm Jay Ogun."- He stepped up and extended his hand- "Officer what can I do to help in this? I have (he thought better of it)– I, I must find her. I need to find her."

Instead of shaking Jay's hand he stepped back and looked at it as if it were dripping in piss.

[Officer1] "And you are? Family, friend, foe?"

Before Jay could respond Joy walked over and placed his hand on Jay's shoulder. Jay closed his eyes and mumbled something before becoming erringly quiet.

[Queen] "Officer ummm- she looked around for his nametag- B.

Tanner, I have no doubt my daughter can take care of herself, but it's not just her out there. We need to know your plans for getting them back- NOW!"

Queen was tired of talking. She wanted the officers to put down their pads, get off the porch, turn on the sirens and take off in the direction of a solution. She needed action-not tension. Joy outstretched his arms and like clockwork his woman fell into them and rested her head. He was bemused he didn't hear any intrusion of someone taking his Princesses. His mind wouldn't allow him to fathom someone getting the better of him.

[**Trish**] "Can you tell us what's next officer B. Tanner?"

[**Officer B. Tanner**] "Oh, it's Bradley." He smiled. "Umm yeah, well, Ms. Sweets it hasn't been 24 hours so we can't really file a missing person report, but for you I plan to jump right on the case. I am personally going to view the front and back porch camera footage."

[**Trish**] "She doesn't have a camera officer Bradley. I hate to say she placed these here to fool folk and it worked until today."

[**Officer Bradley**] "Hmm, she did a good job, but fortunately these are the real things. I can tell by the red light recording us now. I have the same ones. The camera that's seen is a decoy for sure, the real ones are super tiny. They never install one without the other, so I know it's front and back. It seems you're unfamiliar with this knowledge of technology but have no fear because officer Bradley is here" -He chuckled, but no one else laughed. He cleared his throat. - "The cameras cover a nice area of land too. Your friend is smart. Birds of a feather huh-"

He winked at Trish and smiled. Joy broke the awkwardness of their flirtation with a loud sigh. All seemed relieved to know there may be a clue to help but saddened they may not have a way to get to it.

[**Joy**] "But how would we view footage or even know where to go for reviewing if we didn't know about the cameras?"

[Officer Bradley] "That's the good thing about it. The footage is always streaming into a cloud. I can access it."

He ran to the patrol car and pulled out his iPad. He punched in his login information, keyed in some more information and began looking.

Trish was amazed with the initiative of Bradley but disturbed with the silence of the aggressive officer.

[Trish] "Then by all means please, let's look at the footage."

He held out the device motioning everyone to gather around. His partner backed away and stood at the edge of the stairs.

[Officer Bradley] "Let's see at 19:30:06 pm- *Someone dressed in black opens the kitchen door, walks into the kitchen- 19:33:24 pm, the person returns on screen carrying a baby out the kitchen door and placing her into a black car. 19:35:48 pm the person returns carrying a small white cloth in hand. The kitchen door opens, 19:37:06 pm Val's passed out, her mouth covered by the white cloth as she looks lifeless hanging across his shoulder. Hmm, it seems the person tried closing the door but took off running towards the car, throwing Val in before speeding off. 19:39:08 Trish peeps her head out the kitchen door saying something.*

Trish screamed and covered her mouth with her hands. The officer pulled back his iPad and held Trish's shoulder.

[Jay] "What is it?"

[Officer Bradley] "Are you okay?"

[Trish] "I know that car! The plates, can you enlarge it? I know that carrrr!"

Everyone began talking at once asking everything until Bradley put his hands up gesturing time out.

[Officer Bradley] "How do you know the car, and do you know this person? Do you know where they live or why they would want to take your family?"

[Officer1] "Are they lovers?"

He side-eyed Jay. Jay stepped in his face.

[Jay] "Can't you see he damn near had to kill her to get her out. Does this look like a lover of some sort?" Jay stepped closer until he was eye to eye with the aggressive asshole. He wasn't afraid of the big pig wolf. He stepped so close that saliva from Jay's words touched his pale face. "Is it your job to solve crime or cause drama?"

Jay made sure that each word spoken was intentionally dramatic, so he didn't care if he pulled the gun or gaged from being spit on. Bradley placed his hand on his gun and politely asked Jay to back up. The other officer withdrew his gun and aimed it at Jay's head. Joy stepped forth-

[Joy] "Everybody- calm the hell down please! We called y'alll for help and y'all still scared? This is some white shit right here. You act like you can't see this man is hurting and you're contributing with disrespect. C'mon men, my princesses are missing, and we have a possible lead, please focus on saving lives, not destroying or terminating them. Lower your weapon or it can turn very ugly very quickly. We are not afraid, do you understand me?"

Joy's glare and last words rang in their ears like the perfect harmony. It was something about how he said it that they knew they didn't want no smoke. Bradley nodded at his partner and they lowered their weapons. The aggressive officer sucked his teeth then stared at Jay like he was taking a picture for his personal memory bank.

[Officer1] "So, what do y'all do for a living anyways? This is a nice home. I wouldn't expect the likes of – well that's irrelevant. Does anyone have an ID showing this here is indeed your home?"

Trish looked on disapprovingly at Bradley, who dropped his head and motioned for the other officer to be quiet, but he was an arrogant son of a bitch. He pushed Bradley's hand away and kept being an ass..

[Officer1] "I said show me some ID before I call for backup or a morgue. I'll let you darkies decide which you'd like."

[**Jay**] "You called us what now?"

Jay closed his eyes and snapped his fingers. The officer's mouth immediately closed. He looked around wondering what was happening to him as his body and mind moved without warning. He backed away from Jay with both hands stuffed in his pockets. Joy looked on curiously but kept quiet. Bradley apologized for the sudden strange behavior of his partner and extended his hand as if it were an olive leaf. Jay backed away, refusing their touch. Trish was over all the theatrics and tension.

[**Trish**] "It's my neighbor's boyfriend's car, at least that is what it looks like from this end. I would need a larger monitor to be certain."

[**Jay**] "Your neighbor's boyfriend? What the hell does he want with Val?"

Jay became agitated believing enough time had been wasted. He ran down the steps and spoke without turning around

"I will see to it that she returns safely! If they won't"- He pointed at the officers - "I will."

Bradley, still perplexed with his partner's sudden silence, mumbled to him before speaking loud enough for everyone to hear his warning for Jay to be careful. Jay closed his eyes and snapped his finger causing both officers to hold their throat. They looked from one to the other curiously, but couldn't speak. Joy ran to catch Jay.

[**Joy**] "Jay where are you going? And what the hell you got going on baby Thanos? You some type of superhero or some shit?"

Jay didn't respond to the question, but merely cracked a half smile.

[**Jay**] "Please keep me posted. I have to check out some things on my end" - He gave Joy his card with a one shoulder touch hug. - "I'll be back soon."

He whispered something in Joy's ear then got in his metallic blue Maserati and sped off. The officers released their necks and within moments they'd forgotten what just transpired. Instead, they cleared their throats and sang a new tune in attitude and approach.

[**Officer Bradley**] "Ms. Sweet"-

[**Trish**] "Call me Trish."

[**Officer Bradley**] "Okay, Ms. Trish, would you mind following us to the station? I certainly wouldn't mind you riding in the car, but I also understand how unappealing it sounds. I can ask some follow up questions and get some information on your neighbor's friend. Also, we can view the footage from a larger monitor giving you and us certainty of the plates and car."

[**Trish**] "Yes, yes for sure. Anything that can help, I will do! Hey has anyone ever told you you look like the actor ummm- "

[**Officer Bradley**] "Bradley Cooper" Trish shook her head in agreement. "Yes I hear that all the time." He blushed and turned towards the Joys. "You all stay here in case she -he cleared his throat-excuse me, whenever they return. It would be wonderful to have support."

-Bradley extended his hand and Joy shook it. The other officer backed off the porch without saying a word. They turned on their sirens and sped off.

[**Trish**] I'll be back. Hopefully with good news. Call me if they show up before I return."

The Joys waved as Trish took off speeding behind the police car. They heard a thump in the kitchen and Joy took off running, finding nothing except the wind blowing the side door open and closed.

***

Chapter 12

Affirmations and Answers

[Val] "It's okay Ora, mommy got you."
Val held her daughter with patience and paranoia.

"What do you want? Do I know you? Can you remove the blindfolds? Hey, you mind helping, I can't move my legs or open my eyes and I need to see my daughter. She's scared. If you would just allow me to calm her down, please!"

Val inhaled and exhaled deeply. Her tight grip could've been the reason for Ora's discomfort, but she couldn't risk relaxing her hold. With the other hand Val reached in every direction but felt nothing. She thought if she could just grab something- maybe a curtain, the hem of a shirt, or the buckle of a belt. Feeling anything would've helped her identify something and she was desperate. She leaned towards her other senses as the great ancestors taught and began sniffing the air. The smell was familiar, too familiar. She cringed as the aroma of marijuana became overwhelming.

[**Val**] "Who are you?"

She began rubbing the stones of her earrings. She knew there was magic in her imagination and intuition. She imagined herself sitting on a tiny island just small enough to fit her and Light. She sat upright in the chair imagining her knees and toes in the sand. She imagined clear warm water all around believing one false move would drown her. She imagined the water playing between her toes. She wiggled her feet as much as she could, desperate to be anywhere but where she figured she was. She internally prayed on her small island.

[Val] *"Ancestors, Universe, Spirit Guides, and Angels please help me and Light. Because my vision is obstructed, please allow me to secretly hear what's only supposed to be seen. Allow my senses to move about freely since my physical body is bound. Help me as you've always helped before. Activate the energy of each crystal, align me with each stone. Guide and protect us from dangers seen and unseen. I understand darkness can't exist with even a hint of light and I have my Light, so I know we will be victorious in and after this. I call upon you, PLEASSEEEE hear me and answer me expeditiously! Mother Earth, Father Time, and Uncle Wind -blow in blessed answers and blow my burdens away. Protect us from all harm. I am strong. I am courageous. I am brilliant. I am bold. I am ready, I am FREE!."*

Val deeply inhaled and exhaled until Ora began mimicking her breath as normal..

[Ora] "Move it mommy. I wanna see fir eyes."

[**Rage**] "Aye, ya might wanna hold dem dirty hands cuh if she pull again ya gone holla in pain bih. Sum great pain and I'mma let ya suffa with great joy you lyin bihh."

Val felt he was close and thought of grabbing him, but her spirit said to be still and listen intensely. Rage stood tall and blew smoke over Val's head.

[Val] "Can you not do that so close to me and my daughter please?"

Val squirmed in her seat feeling all over Ora's face until she could find Ora's mouth and nose to cover it.

[Val] "Listen, I need to use the bathroom and I'm sure my baby does too. I'm potty training her and she's been doing so well. I don't want to break her routine. Please have mercy and remove this leg contraption along with the blindfold? You can bind me again but allow me this relief."

She knew her daughter was fully potty trained, but she needed a way of escape.

[Rage] "Bihhhh shut upppp!! Yu think ya calling shots? Piss on yo'self -yu 'en da orphan. I'ont give no fuccs- ya 'no whaaa- (he sucked his teeth)-I wasted enuf time. We finna end dis."

He cocked his gun and sat it at Val's temple.

"Ohhh, yu wanna know who I am."

He gripped the blunt with his thumb and finger then pulled until an ash fell at his feet. He began two-stepping from left to right. His shoulders moved up and down in a slow rhythm as he sang his words in the melody of Colors by Ice T.

"I'm ya worse nightmare walking-psychopath talking-Josh all wrapped in one -cuz bihh I been stalking ya. Killa Killa Killa" His laughter filled the room. "It's tyme yu meet ya maker bihh!"

She tightened her eyes behind the blindfold, pulled Ora in close and held her breath.

***

END ......or is it????

This is only the beginning! :-)

I’d like to give you a huge virtual hug and BIG thanks for reading my art. Can you feel it? Of all the books in the world, mine made it into your vision. I feel so blessed and pray this art continues to cross your vision for many years to come. This has been a long time coming and I’m grateful for your patience during the process. You are the reason I keep showing up and believing. Don’t count yourself short because you are making a difference in my world & I love me some you. It's been a long time coming but my change has come, and you know yours is here because we're connected. Hey tribe!! My FAV's!! Everyday I’m rooting4u because I love you. You got this!...

Now, you know it's time for ....

book 2

'Purge'

What Just Happened

Val's usual harmonious breathing had dissonance. Her ears were pounding like heartbeats. She was struggling to stay calm and swallow her own saliva. Her body was wet and she just knew she'd pissed herself, or drowned. Her mind was racing and for a minute she had a crazy thought he'd shot Light first. His fuse was short, if even in existence. She felt comforted in that thought until she didn't. What if he killed Light but decided to let her live and suffer everyday wishing for death. She welcomed the thoughts-no matter how crazy- because any thought was better than the obvious one; time was ticking and hers was just about to timeout.

Rage tapped Val's head with the barrel of the gun before shoving it to her temple. Val let out a short scream before her body became hard as a statue.

He laughed as his trigger finger began to pull, but cursed as his right leg began to shake before his body jerked uncontrollably. The gun slipped from his hand and slammed hard on the floor. Ora's body fell!

www.ingramcontent.com/pod-product-compliance
Lightning Source LLC
LaVergne TN
LVHW010940110826
845149LV00013B/2694